T0142574

FORGEMASTERS OF THE REALM

THE RENDERING WARS

SNÆBJÖRN

Order this book online at www.trafford.com
or email orders@trafford.com

Most Trafford titles are also available at major online book retailers.

Printed in the United States of America.

ISBN: 978-1-4669-8262-8 (sc)
ISBN: 978-1-4669-8264-2 (hc)
ISBN: 978-1-4669-8263-5 (e)

Library of Congress Control Number: 2013903562

Trafford rev. 03/13/2013

 www.trafford.com

North America & international
toll-free: 1 888 232 4444 (USA & Canada)
phone: 250 383 6864 ♦ fax: 812 355 4082

CONTENTS

MAPS

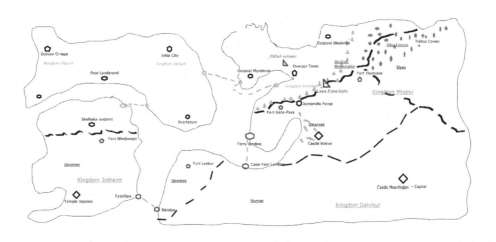

The world of men is coming to a close with old alliances torn, and those which still existed were fragile at best. Trust was displaced with doubts and fear of the scourge that fell from the north. As the inhabitants of the world of men were becoming refugees in their own lands, whole families, cities, shires of the kingdoms were at a loss as to what to expect. With the ever-increasing tides of drumbeats calling for open war, commerce all but stopped. Trade between allies had all but ceased as farms and businesses were boarded up. The legal system came to a halt as soldiering was augmented from the police forces, and the bureaucrats were cowering in hiding. The stench of evil overcame the world; the darkness continued in every nook and cranny. There will be no rest, no safety, no consolation; such is the world as it is now.

The black stallion bore a human toward Fort Dwerbass in a slow gait. The menacing clouds from the north were promising snow as the gales were threating. The ground uttered a grumbling sound as the distant majestic mountain Eldfjall was complaining of a stomachache. He was among a stream of inhabitants trying to get to safety within Fort Dwerbass. The throng of peasants spoke very little as they were laden with everything they could carry. The road, once under good repair, was rutted from the numerous carts and horses, cattle, and other animals. The few that did talk in the caravan of humans and gnomes grumbled about reaching for safety within the fortress walls. Then there were other trains going south, not trusting the defenses of the fort, trying to seek protection and safety in distance.

Soon the masses of inhabitants slowed to a trickle as soldiers directed the refugees to different places within the fort and the village. Single men issued shields, helmets, and swords and directed them to the staging area for combatants. The peasants with families were directed to a place laden with tents.

As the rider of the black stallion reached a stationed soldier at the checkpoint, he was asked his business. He told the soldier that he was on official business and wished to talk to the commander Baldur.

"Sire, Baldur is no more commander . . . you need speak with Lieutenant Foringi. But he is busy," stated the soldier. He instructed him to proceed toward the command post, and the nameless rider complied with the instruction.

"Here be, take a helmet and sword," stated the sentry as he offered his booty.

The nameless rider of the black stallion waved off the offerings saying, "Nay, I shall not have any use of these things." He dismounted and proceeded toward the command post with his steed in tow.

The rider of the black stallion addressed the sentry on duty and was escorted into the command post. Lieutenant Foringi stood before him in a stately stance, which showed an air of professionalism as he greeted the older gentleman.

"Sire, I wish to know of the fortunes of Baldur. He is a friend and close companion," stated the stranger.

The lieutenant scanned the man, a gray old man dressed in gray garments as a mage. In his right hand he held a brown staff with a huge diamond atop.

"He is no longer serving here at Fort Dwerbass. Perchance I can assist you?" asked Lieutenant Foringi. "Do I know you?" added the lieutenant.

"Nay, but can you tell me where he is? Forgive me, I am rude. I am Helgi the Gray," replied Helgi as he bowed slightly toward the lieutenant.

"The last time I heard from Baldur, he was in Castle Hearthglen, but I was informed that I am the commander of the fort," stated Foringi, adding, "Queen's orders."

Helgi sensed that the answer was troublesome. "Do you know if he has been reassigned to another post?"

"Nay, I not know. In times, normally when officers are reassigned, it is public knowledge . . . but in these times," continued Foringi. "What is your business with Baldur? Perchance I can offer assistance to you, Helgi the Gray!"

"Nay, but I thank you for your offer to me. Do you know where a gnome called Gagns can be located?" inquired Helgi.

Helgi was directed toward the newly erected Tent City, where Gagns was helping feed the newcomers. Soon he found him dressed in an apron and sporting a chef's hat and preparing some lamb stew. Outside of the humorous appearance, he found Gagns little changed since the last time he saw him. Clearing his throat, Helgi said, "Ahem, greetings, my old friend."

Without looking up, Gagns squeaked, "Y-y-you need t-to get in l-line."

"Forgive me, I need information of Baldur and Biggy," interjected Helgi, to which Gagns turned around and examined the old man in front of him.

Suddenly, as if a light of recognition had turned on, Gagns stammered, "Snjofell . . . w-w-where is my b-brother? And why are you dressed in g-g-gray . . . and your staff, it is different too!"

Laughing, Helgi bowed at the hip and said, "Snjofell is no more. I am now known as Helgi the Gray. I'm at your service. Perhaps we should go to Boars Inn and speak privately."

Boars Inn had not changed, except for the throng of people inside. Part of it had been converted to assist with the newcomers. Gagns and Helgi found their way into the kitchen where a sequestered area afforded some privacy. Gagns had removed his apron and hat and started to hammer questions on Helgi. Holding a hand up as a signal that Gagns was to slow down, Helgi recounted the events in Jarnsmiða Forge, how he had defeated the [1] einauga by ramming his staff into the eye.

Gagns was awestruck, so much so that he forgot to stammer. "You are one of the gods !" acclaimed Gagns incredibly.

Laughing out loud, Helgi responded, "Nay, I be not a god. I am as mortal as you. Let us say that I have a different station in life. But I know not of Agnar nor Biggy. I was hoping that you could provide answers. More importantly, what has befallen Baldur?"

---

[1] Einauga: A cyclops-type of creature that had died with Snjofell in the pit of the Jarnsmiða Forge.

Gagns shook his shoulders and replied, "I heard n-n-nothing. Now ye b-b-be starting to s-s-scare me."

"How well do you know Lieutenant Foringi? I feel that we need to enlist his help to find Baldur," said Helgi.

In response, Gagns replied, "He is n-n-no Baldur, but he i-i-i-is a good l-l-leader. He a-a-appreciates (appreciates) my help in t-t-the fort. I trust him, and t-the fort is in g-good hands."

Helgi commanded, "Well, then if you consider him as trustworthy, then let us not waste time!" To that, they took leave from Boars Inn and sought out Foringi.

Jarnsmiða Forge was a formidable place to be—dark, dank, wet, and obnoxious ruins. The city walls were damp and slimy to the touch, and the stench of rot permeated the ruin. In front of them were tunnels leading where only the gods knew.

"Where now?" asked Dabs.

There were signs chiseled on the walls, but no one could read the runic inscriptions. After the narrow escape from the drawbridge and the jaunt walking for over an hour, Agnar suggested that they take a break, eat some food, and try to figure what next to do. All were agreed and shared broken flaxen bread, divided up, which they ate.

"We need to refill the lambskin jugs with water. There are a few places where water is seeping from the damaged walls," added Biggy.

SiSi had not left the side of Biggy as they smiled toward each other. Smari stood up, and using one of the jugs, walked toward the flowing water. Without warning, the ground swayed and shook—another tremor. Smari regained his footing, and the jug was soon filled.

"Well, any suggestion?" asked Dabs. "The door to the right seems wider than the rest. I think we can assume the smaller doorways lead to tunnels."

"Aye, I agree then," piped in Biggy. "Should we be off? I would like some fresh air and see the stars in the night skies again, and soon too."

As the troop entered the right door, Dabs suddenly whispered back, "Tracks in the dust. They aren't human but not animal either. Agnar, grab more torches there on the wall. We will be needed them." Agnar complied with the request and returned with two torches. "I nary can tell what type of tracks they are."

Agnar knelt on one knee and tried to ascertain the type of tracks they were. As a trained hunter, he was best suited to decipher the tracks. "Hmm, I think they are goblin, but they are old," replied Agnar. "I not know of any goblins in the dwarven realm . . . will be curious to find out what they are. *Komdu*," he instructed his sekhmet to appear. Bangsi appeared instantly and began to sniff the tracks.

SiSi added, "Goblins, we know not of goblins in the mountains. I hope this dunna be bad fortunes for us." She threw a glaring eye toward Agnar.

Going through the doorway, the group met stairsteps leading downward. Agnar ordered Bangsi to scout down the steps, and the sekhmet soon returned a signal that it was safe. SiSi, with torch in hand, blinked down the staircase and yelled back,

"Looks like we are on a lower level. I see another door ahead. But be careful as the steps may be slippery or damaged from the tremors."

One by one they descended until they reached SiSi. A few of the stone steps crumbled, throwing some debris downward. The staircase held though, and the group continued the descent as the light from the torches was swallowed by the darkness behind them. The staircase was narrow but not cramped. Holding up toward the wall, they found crude etchings of dwarfs and what was depicted as a forge. "We are probably on the right path at least," said Dabs.

Beyond the door was a ledge leading to more doors, more likely more tunnels, and in the room was another staircase leading down. Repeating the scouting session as before, SiSi announced to the group that the same scenery was before them. Descending cautiously, the company reassembled at the bottom of the staircase. This, however, was unlike other levels; this one had giant konglo eggs and webs from the ceiling to the floor.

Biggy cautioned under his breath, "T his be the queen's nest, and we should retreat slowly."

The team agreed and slowly started to back away. Among some of the web casings they found skeletal remains and partial bodies, some dwarven and others of goblins.

Biggy rummaged through his rucksack and pulled out a [2]training rod. Whispering to the group, he said, "Dunno come in here until I tell ye. The queen will swarm us if ye enter. I be all right, remember, I trained and owned konglos." Biggy crept forward toward the door with torch in hand, and looking back, he raised a hand ordering them to be silent. Inside were a slew of old and newly spun webbings. He looked for the queen web spindle as he adjusted his eyes to the dark beyond the light from the torch. Over him was the queen, crouched in the corner near the ceiling. "Found her!" said Biggy to himself.

The queen was massive, every bit twice the size of Biggy, with huge jaws and wire-sized hairs on her legs, and was giving off a sound like a small pig squeal. He gently strummed the web spindle like a strum of a fiddle and caused her to shuffle toward Biggy. When she was at the right distance from him, he raised his training rod and started to tame the animal. The queen konglo was bathed with an aqua-velvet light from the training rod. With that, she opened her gaping jaws, getting ready to spit a web around him. Biggy easily avoided it as he blinked away at the right time and continued with the rod, exercising the rod and synchronizing the swaying of the konglo with the rod. Again she attacked, trying to shoot a web to encapsulate Biggy, with no success.

---

[2] Training rods are used by ferreters (hunter military specialty) to tame wild creatures. The creatures are usually cats, spiders, bears, wolves, etc.

Then, with no warning, the volcano started trembling again! Biggy fell to the ground, right into a web on the ground ! The queen sensed the prey was about to be dinner and pounced. A look of fear showed for a moment in SiSi, and her exhalation from breathing was from bated breath. Luckily, the tremor was just a single ripple. Biggy blinked and appeared behind the queen with training rod in hand. He was covered with silvery webbing, and he had to brush the strands from his eyes. Looking into the eyes of the queen konglo, he continued to tame the beast. She retreated, followed by a charge, and gave a small grunt as if she were saying, "What is this thing?" And soon the ordeal was over. Biggy had tamed the queen and returned to the group.

SiSi ran toward him, brushing the cocoon webbings from Biggy and said, "Well, I need to teach ye some manners, eh?" She was obviously proud of him and winked an eye at him.

"I told ye I be good with konglos," stated Biggy, his chest swelling with pride. "And dunno touch any of the eggs, she will attack us without warning! The other worker konglos won't bother us as long as the queen is tamed."

The troop continued through the queen's nest after the queen konglo had been instructed to stay. The smell was terrible with the stench of decaying bodies and such. They proceeded through most of the passageways, constantly brushing webbings from their bodies. They all laughed after they looked at themselves—dirty, covered in webs, and they found it humorous seeing each other. The path was covered with skulls, bones, and worms, centipedes, scorpions, and bats soared near the ceiling. Biggy cursed lightly under his breath, saying, "Creatures from 'ell if ye ask me. Cannah stand 'em."

Finally the group reached the end of the hallway and met a staircase down, but this time a single door. They descended the staircase and reached the bottom. The group could sense a slight increase of temperature and the smell of sulfur. At the bottom, they converged toward a stone-hewn door, which apparently had not been opened for several hundred years. Bangsi started to snarl as if it was alert to danger. The group armed themselves as Attafæt was summoned. It took all the strength of both Dabs and Agnar to budge the door. Beyond the door, they were stunned by lit torches on the walls, and standing before them were goblins!

The iron boats were proceeding as planned, and King Magnus was pleased. In the industrial room located in Jarnsmiða are parts scattered here and there, as the construction is done in sections. King Magnus smiled toward Gormur, the lead engineer for the project.

"Nicely done, well done," complimented Magnus to Gormur. "When will the first one be ready for trial runs?"

"Not for another six to eight fortnights," replied Gormur. "We still need to build the steam generators, not to mention the coal bins needed for the generators. But the iron boats—I call 'em [3] Skjaldbak with iron scales—won't be able to carry many soldiers or weapons for making war, only three blunderbusses."

"Continue as you are," instructed Magnus as he returned to the throne room. Magnus was greeted by one of his counselors, and he asked the counselor, "What news?"

---

[3] Skaldabokum: an iron boat that is similar to a turtle once submerged.

"Sire, may I suggest? We have received some rumors that Fort Hermana to the east is running on low supplies, and some hoarding has started. Should we make sure our grains and such are in good order within our city? I'm sure we have plenty, but if a sudden onslaught of refugees shows up, it could catch us unawares," said the adviser.

King Magnus considered for a moment then stated, "Yes, yes, and warn the populace not to hoard things. After all, we are not in an open war . . . yet. Prepare the caverns below for shelter if need be."

"I will carry out your wishes, sire. It is rumored that Castle Hearthglen is feeling the pinch now that the farmers are fleeing to safer areas. I even heard that a bureaucrat was slain when a mob of city dwellers was attempting to hoard foodstuffs," continued the adviser.

"As I, the leader of the dwarfs, decree that, until further notice, all stately banquets will be cancelled effectively immediately," ordered the king. "I know that we, the people within this kingdom, nary can be relied upon neither for Castle Hearthglen nor for our safety and security. The dwarven race must be protected by dwarfs, not the race of men."

When the adviser left, a scowl came upon the king. "Perhaps I should attend to the city defenses myself," thought Magnus. He walked about the castle yard, inspecting the catapults on the outer walls, talking with the sentries, and asking their opinions. He examined the oil vats and giant crossbow arrows, not wanting to be caught off guard. "No enemy has ever breached the city. I pray the day will never come," the king said to himself.

As he continued walking through the trade center, he observed that the city populace was going about business as usual. The king sensed a change of attitude among the population. The inhabitants were full aware of the dangers that faced the kingdom. It wasn't panic or a feeling of despair; it was an intangible feeling, perhaps caution. He thought a moment of Snjofell and Dabs, wondering how their quest progressed. "At least no news is good news," thought the king.

The queen granted an audience to be heard. Helgi, Gagns, and Foringi were waiting for the announcement that they could enter. Before gaining entry, the sentries demanded that they must be disarmed. Gagns and Commander Foringi relinquished their swords while Helgi stated that he was just an old man, not armed. When the sentry asked for the staff, Helgi replied with "You wouldn't want to deprive me of my cane, I need it for walking." The sentry thought about it for a moment then said, "You may pass then." After a few moments, the sentries announced, "Enter."

As they entered the throne room, the queen Audri was seated on the throne, looking frail and old in appearance. Her face was lined with creases, and her eyes were glassy. To her right sat Ormskepna. The announcer cried out, "Introducing Helgi the Gray and Commander Foringi from Fort Dwerbass." The trio bowed as a courtesy and proceeded toward the queen. Suddenly, she sat up at attention, shouting, "Snjofell—you are not welcome here!" Instantly, Ormskepna leapt to his feet as his smirking features changed to fear after hearing that.

Immediately, Helgi lowered his staff toward the queen, commanding, "Ormskepna, you fool. Begone with your cursed spell!" And his staff sang a bolt of lightning toward the queen.

Simultaneously, both Foringi and Gagns accosted Ormskepna, wielding a hidden dagger and threatening him. The queen slumped back into the throne, shook a moment, and fell into slumber for a second. Within seconds, the creases within her face disappeared; her glassy-eyed stare was replaced with clear, intelligent eyes. For a second she seemed to be confused, but then started to gain her presence. Turning toward Ormskepna, the queen slapped him, knocking him to the floor. The responding sentries who had entered the throne room were astounded when she yelled toward them, "Seize him!" pointing toward Ormskepna. "I'll listen no more to the lies from you"

Ormskepna was groveling on the floor and beseeching the queen as the sentries stood him on his feet. "What should I do with you? Execute you as a traitor?" the queen asked. Ormskepna started to plea with the queen, but she did not want to bother and responded with "SILENCE!"

Helgi interjected, "Nay, your majesty, do not lower your level to him. May I suggest that he should be horse-tied, turned loose into the Lava-Gate Pass. If the northern alliance will have him, they will let him live, else if he should die, his death would be on their hands, not ours."

The queen then commanded, "Let it be so!" As they watched, the captive was dragged out, the queen then realized, "My daughter . . . release Lady Zonda and Baldur and the others we have imprisoned wrongly!"

Turning toward the trio, the queen wept as she realized how much she had damaged the realm. She slumped into the throne teary eyed. "I have been blinded by foolish counsel . . . I feel shame. Please allow me to right my wrongs."

"I am Helgi the Gray. I offer my services to the queen. Snjofell as you knew him is no more. And may I introduce Commander Foringi and the little one, Gagns." Helgi bowed and added, "I beseech you not dwell on past events. We have much to do and little time to do it."

The detained prisoners were led out of the dungeon into the open air. All of them were affected by the sunlight, causing them to squint and rub their eyes. The sentries were bombarded with questions from the prisoners demanding to know where they were going. The prisoners were met with silence and told not to speak to the guards. With the shackles gone, they stretched their arms and legs, enjoying the freedom of movement. They were enjoying basking in the sunlight as the skies were cloudless and temperatures were cool but not cold. Soon they were led into the guardhouse where they were instructed to clean themselves up and returned their clothing to them. They were all wearing puzzled looks on their faces with questions in their eyes. Of course, the guards were mute, leaving all questions unanswered.

Baldur asked the prisoners if they could speak, to which he was told that they could; however, the guards will not answer any questions. Baldur espied Stephan and approached him with an extended hand to greet him. With him was one of the dwarfs in the last cell, whose name Baldur found out was Rikard, a ferreter by trade.

"What has happened here? Are we finally free? Has the queen died or been deposed?" asked Baldur to Stephan.

"I know not of what has happened. Perchance we will be fodder for the amusement of the guards," replied Stephan.

Turning to Rikard, Baldur asked, "Perchance you know of Agnar, a ferreter like you. How long have you been in the dungeon?"

"Aye, I know of him. I served with him a few years ago. I think he has a sekhmet as a wolverine," declared Rikard. "He is half-human, half-elf, if I recollect. I spent seven years in the hole. You were lucky."

"Yes, yes, he is the one. He served time under my command at Fort Hermana." Baldur smiled. "He was an excellent soldier. I intend to find out why we were jailed. I won't rest without some answers."

The group of prisoners were smiling and laughing once they realized they were going to be freed. To a man they were almost gaunt and tired-looking. Some of them had been in the dungeon, years mostly for petty crimes or being disloyal to the realm.

The commander of the guards approached Baldur and said, "The queen requests your appearance. You are to come with me."

"What does the queen want with me?" asked Baldur. "It seems like she isn't dead . . . I need some answers."

"You will get answers to your questions soon enough. I am returning your armor, but you need to clean yourself up first," instructed the commander. "Make yourself suitable before you show yourself to the queen!"

Baldur turned to Stephan and Rikard, shrugged his shoulders, and raised his eyebrows. "Very well, I will want to get to the bottom of this."

"You, men, feed yourselves. I have some real food for you in the guardhouse. And when you are finished, wash yourselves and then rest up. There are real beds there too." The commander smirked.

The commander of the guards escorted Baldur to the palace grounds where he was given back his armor, which he donned. The grounds were adorned with various trees of oranges, pears, and apples. It was tended by gardeners and kept up immaculately. Baldur found it ironic that such good care was taken with the garden while beneath them was misery in cells. When Baldur finished cladding his armor, the commander said, "I shall return your sword. I warn you, keep it sheathed. I know not what our queen wants with your appearance, but we will protect the queen."

As the duo neared the throne door to the palace, a sentry snapped to and opened the door. As they entered, Baldur was stunned—before him were the queen, Zonda, Gagns, Foringi, and someone resembling Snjofell. But Snjofell was different, not the Snjofell he recalled. To the left of the queen sat Zonda, beaming of smiles and laughing with the queen. The queen was sitting on her throne, but she was totally different too in attitude, smiling and laughing, and her appearance looked years younger with bright, lucid eyes. "Why is fair-haired Lady Zonda sitting on the throne area? Where is Ormskepna? And how come did Snjofell and Gagns and Foringi appear before the queen?" A befuddled Baldur was full of questions and thoughts.

The ruler of the Gnomish Realm, King Smakongur, was pondering about the almost daily occurrences of the incursions from the north. His ruling clique, who numbered only four gnomes, was clamoring for a solution. The trespassers, mostly Ápstiler, Orcs, and some trolls, had stepped up their jaunts within the territory, leaving destruction in the form of killings and thievery. While the problem was not considered an act of war, rather as a nuisance, King Smakongur, like all ruling elites, had distaste for change. The counsel, along with King Smakongur, had decided that the local police would handle it and not the sentry patrols from Fort Windswept. The counsel dispatched a messenger to advise the changes. After all, the fort was the cause of the problem. The realm had good relations with the neighbors, and they wanted to keep it that way. A few minor occurrences, which is what it was called. That pesky race of men—and the fort was manned by men—they were the obstacle in the north. Changes had come upon the realm, and the ruling elites turned a blind eye in store for more change for the worse for the Gnomish Realm.

Stunned was the word to describe the five adventurers, and more stunned were the goblins. The entrance to the old castle and forge had never seen anyone enter this far; some straggler konglos, Orcs, and goblins, but no people of the dwarven race and definitely not gnomes and elves. The encounter between the goblins and intruders left them staring at each other. No words were spoken. The greenish goblins, with round eyes like egg yolks, sparse hair upon their heads, and elongated fingers with long fingernails, were laughable to the appearance. Outside of Dabs and Agnar, the other members of the team had never seen a live goblin before. The armed group, with Bangsi and Attafæt in the troop, kept the goblins, numbered at about forty, at bay with fear in their eyes.

Dabs broke the silence with "We mean you no harm. But if you attack, we will defend ourselves." Silence was the response. After a pregnant moment of minutes, "I am Dabbilus of the Forge-Master clan. I seek the forge below. I come in peace." Nothing was heard from the goblins, which had amassed before them. Noticing that the goblins seemed to eye Attafæt and Bangsi, Dabs instructed Biggy and Agnar to tell the sekhmets with the group to leave. The adventurers sheathed their weapons and gasps could be heard from the goblins, and suddenly, an air of pleasances appeared, changing the atmosphere within the group of goblins.

"No orc, orc bad. Orc eat darlings. I no hurt. I be good." Suddenly, a goblin broke the silence. "Come, father, come, darlings," he beckoned with a long finger. A massive wave of goblins broke, allowing the team to enter the huge cavern area. "You come . . . come, father," repeated the instruction. The speaking goblin approached Dabs, extending his hand upon Dabs's shoulder.

His skinny green skin, sharp teeth, sparse thin hairs upon his head caused Dabs to momentarily be vigilant. "So you don't like orcs, that's a good start. We will follow you."

Dabs and his team soon fell in with the leader of the goblins, distrustfully so, but they did agree to follow them. The cavern was massive, with torches mounted on the walls every twenty-five paces. The path was well-worn, which dispelled any thoughts of getting lost. Every now and then, they could detect old runic writings on the wall. Agnar removed his warming cape as the air in the area was warm, and the stench of sulfur surrounded their nostrils. After marching for about half an hour, the lead goblin broke the silence by saying, "Here, father, come," to no one in particular. Beyond his extended arm was a living area similar to Castle Jarnsmiða, obviously made by dwarfs. The lead goblin broke into a trot, leading the team into a pleasant dwelling.

"Father, darlings, here!" the goblin yelled in an excited pitch for the inhabitants to greet his guests. Hopping around in a state of enthusiasm, arms flailing, he repeated, "Father, father, father," in an attempt to get the attention of the event of the newcomer's arrival.

The troop noticed goblins at the windows as the villagers were investigating what the commotion was about. All of a sudden, Dabs gasped, "By the gods, dwarfs here too," as he espied some dwarfs looking out the windows! Soon, an elderly dwarf exited the building, and it was apparent that he was as shocked as the team was. He rubbed his eyes in disbelief, seeing a dwarf among the five newcomers, gnomes, and an elf! Stroking his belly-long beard, he blurted out, "Dost mine eye deceive me? How ye come to be here?"

Dabs approached the old dwarf with an extended hand and stated, "Dabbilus, paladin by trade, of the Forge-Masters clan, and Agnar, ferreter by trade, of the forest elves; Biggy, farmer by trade, of the gnomes; Smari, my valet; and SiSi, tradesman from the Castle Vokva."

Caught off guard, the elderly dwarf shook Dabs's hand and said, "Forgive me manners. I be Loftur Hamarsson of Jarnsmiða Forge of the Flame-Keepers clan! By the gods, how be ye here? How did you escape the Einauga and the konglos and the Orcs?"

Smiling and with a twinkle in his eye, Dabs answered, "Aye, terrible trek, and the human of the group perished as well as the Einauga. And the purpose of our journey was to find the Great Forge."

Agnar interrupted and added, "The world as we know it is coming to an end. The demons of the north, the orcs, the trolls, the Ápstil and the goblins have waged war upon us. But you have goblins here, and this is strange, to put it mildly."

"Please, please do come in, and we talk in pleasant surroundings," said Loftur, "an'a dine with us, for it is a festive occasion. 'N aye wanna greet me li'l lady. SiSi, is it your name? Misses willa have lots of questions, and ye will like her."

Loftur accommodated his guests well, and the dinner was fabulous as the group had nothing to eat but the bread and water. His wife, Sigurlaug, and four children, two boys and two girls in their late teens, were affable. The group instantly grew a bond between them. Loftur explained how they had been hiding among the caverns when the castle was attacked and how they had to seal up the entrances to avoid egress for the orcs, einauga, and konglos. Biggy and Agnar captivated the two boys, talking about their military service and how the villages, forts, and castles were populated with humans, gnomes, dwarfs, and elves. The boys had never seen the world outside of the forge, and they hammered Agnar and Biggy with questions. SiSi, as with Biggy and Agnar, felt as at home with Sigurlaug and talked endlessly of Castle Vokva and women talk. Loftur and Dabs were engrossed in talk of the Orcs, of how the goblins had wandered into the caverns and befriended them, and of the quest, and Loftur was intrigued of it. Loftur agreed to show them to the forge but also told Dabs that the forge had not been used for many years. He didn't even know if it would work again.

Eventually, Loftur was asked how to escape the Jarnsmiða Forge and what will be the fate of those remaining once the mountain blew up. He beseeched Loftur and the inhabitants to flee to Castle Vokva and start a new life among the world of people again, to which he said that the decision must be a group decision as the darlings were his family now. Loftur bid good-night to the team and said that tomorrow the work will commence.

Baldur was at a loss. After all, he had vowed to get some answers and to find out who or what was behind the situation concerning Baldur and his fellow prisoners. Now, he was dumbfounded, and the millions of questions were limitless. Pursing his lips and raising a questioning eyebrow to Snjofell, he was speechless for a moment.

"Snjofell, Gagns, Lieutenant . . . what is happening?" asked Baldur.

Smiling, Helgi the Gray stated, "Ahh, yes, yes. All in due time your questions will be answered. Come forth. I am no more known as Snjofell, and I will explain it for you, but first, I am Helgi the Gray, at your service," bowing slightly toward Baldur, "Our regal queen has, shall I say . . . uh, a change of attitude. But you need to send your questions directly to the queen and at the proper time and place. Much has transpired recently, and the realm needs you at your place. Gagns and the lieutenant have done a wonderful job in your absence."

Baldur sneaked a glance toward the queen and Lady Zonda, to which Lady Zonda intercepted. "Sire

Baldur, let me and my mother, the queen, offer apologies for what has transpired of recent."

Baldur was floored. "Your *mother* is the queen . . . now *I'm* really confused. H-h-h-h-how—," Baldur stammered.

Queen Audri then cut Baldur short as he was talking and said, "Your loyalty to the realm, your honesty, and courage to your duties are beyond reproach. I have heard much about you, and from allies and colleagues, not from disloyal counsel." Baldur caught a glimpse of Lady Zonda as she blushed lightly at the words from Queen Audri. "Therefore, I know men of your stature, and we need such men of you within the ranks of the realm. I will atone for the disservice you have been under for the last few weeks. I then propose that you accept a new post within the realm, the rank of commander of Realm Guards, in charge of the realm, answering only to me. Agreed?"

Baldur's head was swimming, unable to think as fast as the events that occurred in the audience chamber. "If I be bold, I counterpropose that I will accept the position only on one provision: restore all my fellow prisoners' records, expunge their wrongs, return them back to their ranks and duties and their honor. If you do that, I gladly will be under your service once more."

Lady Zonda could not hide her swelling pride in Baldur. Lady Zonda turned her head toward her as if to pray that her mother will accept.

Queen Audi then expounded, "Be it done! Guards, spread the word that Sire Baldur now commands the realm. Baldur, come forth and be knighted for your service to the realm."

All those in attendance in the audience chamber were beaming with pride to watch Baldur walk slowly and kneel before the queen. She held Baldur's sword aloft, lightly tapping each shoulder and pronounced, "You are to be known as Sir Baldur forevermore. I knight you as Sir Baldur! You may now stand before your queen."

Baldur took her extended wrist and kissed it. Baldur looked toward Lady Zonda and smiled deeply, his clear blue eyes looking deeply into hers.

The queen then said, "Audience is now closed. Everyone in attendance here be at the Royal Ballroom this evening." Looking toward Baldur, she added, "And the former prisoners are to attend as well."

The evening was delightful. At the head of the table was the queen, to the right was Lady Zonda, and to the left was Baldur. Of course, Commander Foringi (Baldur had promoted him to commander and designated Gagns as honorable lieutenant of the fort), Helgi the Gray, and the former prisoners were dispersed throughout the table. After the dinner, the queen asked Baldur to speak to the group.

Standing up with mug in hand, Baldur said, "I salute you. I see before me the finest people. I honor you. May our queen be blessed with loyal and humble patriots. To you, Commander Rikard, I wish you to become the commander of Fort Gate-Pass. We need to start to behave as soldiers. Soon, open war will be upon us, and you are a fine soldier. To you, Commander Stephan, I desire you to command Fort Windswept and take a squad of 120 to be garrisoned in the fort. Commander Foringi, return with Lieutenant Gagns and one hundred men to garrison there. I am now ordering all males fifteen years of age and older to be conscripted. I will not allow the dark hordes of the north to take us by surprise. I have instructed the castle guards to root out the known spies which have infested us for too long. Helgi the Gray will be my deep personal counsel and may wander without interference within the realm. To the other guests here tonight, you have done your duties to the throne. Should you be willing, you will be most welcome, but you are of no obligation to serve again. We will not think of you unkindly should you wish to leave the service of the realm."

Baldur returned to his seat and everyone stood up and applauded. Baldur blushed and motioned for everyone to sit, but they stood. To a man, they nodded their heads in agreement and said, "Sir Baldur, I pledge to serve you honestly and honorably."

Baldur was almost in tears, tears of joy, and croaked in a shaky voice, "Thank you, you are beyond honorable. May I be honorable to each of you."

The queen then stood up, clapped her hands, and commanded, "Let the music play," to which the band began to exercise their instruments.

Later in the evening, the ales and wines flowing, a messenger approached Sir Baldur. He had a missive from Fort Windswept in which they had been ordered to cease all patrols along the north border. Baldur, with a grim look on his face, turned to Helgi the Gray and the queen and showed them the message. "So, it soon starts," was the utterance from Baldur. He pulled Commander Stephan aside and ordered that his troops leave tomorrow for Fort Windswept. "A dire ending for a wonderful evening," surmised Baldur under his breath.

Svaramin was staring intently within the orb he used for scrying. His hawkish nose was almost upon the orb, and his thin lips were fogging the orb. He was trying to confirm the intelligence coming back from his spies around Fort Windswept. With a smile on his face, Svaramin was pleased to see that there were no patrols in the area, and he saw that there was no evidence of horses or men displaying any signs of any patrols. Svartaturn will dispatch a wyvern messenger to Ormur, perhaps to suggest a different plan. "If Fort Windswept was just an easy target, like a bloated tick on the landscape, maybe we could launch a first strike in the north of Jotheim. I need to talk with Ormur, start to send reinforcements now to Skelbaka Outpost. The odds of the little useless gnomes resisting us would be overwhelming by our side." Laughing out loud, he added, "That fat, lazy, double-chinned King Smakongur was indeed humorous to look at."

In his sick mind, Svaramin was thinking of how good he would feel to watch Orcs eat him if he were to be captured, the cowardly tub of lard. "Our reinforcements had reached the ready state. The trolls had increased around the Lava-Gate Pass area, and with the muscle power of the trolls, we can open the Lava Gates as they have not been opened for centuries. Soon, within a few weeks, the weather will be favorable for an attack. If we can concrete our positions in the area of Fort Hermana, we can crush the puny race of men once and for all."

Salim-Dug had done an excellent job of working with the spy network. He intended to let Ormur know about his work. The dwarfs, though, might be a problem, but with Ormurs overwhelming forces, the dwarfs could hold out for a week, maybe two weeks.

Svaramin walked to the rooftop of Svartaturn and surveyed the landscape around the tower. The incubators had been in overdrive, producing thousands of orc-embryo sacs. The majestic Eldfjall was still spewing black ash, clouds, and steam, creating a background for the wyvern patrols, which were aloft. Svaramin turned his thoughts to Helgi the Gray. He was a player in the game of life, just as Svaramin. Though they were on the opposite sides, he still considered Helgi the Gray to be a friend. Countless times over the ages, they both tested metals upon each other, and they will be combatants in the future. The gods will ensure that if either of them perishes, they will resurrect the combatant. Perhaps it was the will of the gods that both are mortal, but their souls use mortals as containers of mortal bodies.

"Yes, we will meet countless times in the future, perhaps not as Svaramin and Helgi the Gray, but we will meet again. We are the referees in the game of life, we keep the rules in the universe, good versus evil, like the night skies counterbalance the sunlight skies," thought Svaramin. He amused himself with the idea. "Soon, our enemies will feel our wrath!"

Toward the forge, the band of adventurers left the old castle ruins with Loftur and a few darlings leading the way.

"Finally, making progress," remarked Dabs with Biggy. After a fine night's rest and full bellies, Biggy smiled broadly.

"Aye, nice to have a full night's sleep too," retorted Biggy.

"Well, I for one will feel better once we can restart the Great Forge," added Agnar. "How far do we have to go now?"

Loftur replied, "Maybe half hour of walking. But keep an open eye for Orcs and goblins. Dey be of the north, not the darlings here. Dey sometimes be lookin' fer anything dey can steal."

The cavern narrowed and wormed off to the right, but it was obviously well traveled by Loftur, darlings, and Orcs. Dabs and Smari had equipped themselves with skin jugs, used for water to forge the ore. Smari was humored to see, upon eyeing the load he carried, that it was larger than he was. SiSi was holding Biggy's hand as they trooped onward with the group.

Shortly, Loftur put a hand up to signal caution as he neared a huge boulder. "Shh, we needa be careful here . . . we dunna wanna to be seen." He crept forward as the party remained hidden by the boulders. Whispering, Loftur said, "Here orcs camp sometimes in this area." After scouting the area, he signaled for the troop to come forward. There was evidence of small campfires just ahead, two or three days old. Up ahead was a huge doorway that led to the Great Forge. "To the right side of the cavern, just beyond other boulders, ye can find water."

Dabs took command and said, "Let us see what we need to do to get it working again. SiSi, thee needa keep an eye open for the ward-stones placed to dam up the lava. Use your magic and dispel any ward-stones. Thou, thee, and Smari can carry water. Agnar, use your sekhmet and man guard-duty. Biggy, you work the bellows. Everyone ready?" With a deep breath, everyone headed for the entrance, not knowing what they will find.

Agnar beckoned his sekhmet, Bangsi, and instructed him to scout the interior of the forge room in case any surprise was to befall the assembled band. Soon Bangsi returned, indicating that the room had not any unusual creatures, Orcs, or the like. With an exhalation of relief, SiSi took charge of the room, scanning for any ward-stones.

She found the room to be rather large, with no extra doors but with an extremely high ceiling. In the center of the room lay the Great Forge, cold and silent. On top of the forge extended the hat, or hood, that was used to exhaust the fumes. It appeared to be made of gold or some pyrite-like substance. On the right wall, piercing the ceiling from top to bottom, were displayed the flue pipes, a drum-sized apparatus obviously constructed from stone. The pipe ran down into the forge where the lava was to be used for forging. The exhaust pipes went to the opposite wall and up back into the ceiling. Closing her eyes, SiSi extended her arms toward the flue pipe and then concentrated on the exhaust pipe. She completed the scans and said, "I 'ave located one, to the ceiling, right wall. 'Tis a ward-stone pushing like an invisible thumb to plug up the hole, holding the lava flow back. I suggest Smari examine the pipes before I disenchant the ward-stone." She had turned toward Dabs to seek other instructions.

"Excellent. Smari, give thine a diagnosis," ordered Dabs and took a step aside to allow Smari full access to the room. "Looks like we have plenty of space to be inside, but once the forge gets hot, it will get plenty warm in there."

Agnar had completed the search of the cavern around the Great Forge as it was a circular room made of stone. Two doors were beyond the rear of the forge chambers, but nothing was found out of order. Bangsi was posted to the right rear door, and Agnar positioned himself near the left rear door of the chamber.

Smari retrieved his tinker's tools from his knapsack and completed his task within ten minutes.

"Seems like it will hold, but I canna say if any damages are in the other pipes. Looks like these are like any heitapipur in use today." He looked toward Dabs for further instructions.

"Well, SiSi, 'tis now up to you to restart the forge! Need anything before thee start?" asked Dabs in a guarded tone.

"Nay, but ye guys keep quiet, and don't interrupt the spell for no reason. And leave ye the room, donna wanna molten lava splashing around," she said, waiting for each person to nod in agreement.

Leaving the crowd behind, she entered the Great Forge room and situated herself in the center, with one hand on her hip and the other extended toward the flue pipe near the ceiling. Within seconds, her body began to twitch and sway as if being stung by bees. Suddenly, the molten lava began to flow downward, filling the flue pipes; she watched the forge container fill with dancing flames, and liquid lava came alive. The forge came alive again, singing once again after having been silent for ages! The heat in the chamber rose almost immediately and caused the party to step back.

A teary-eyed Dabbilus, a member of the Forge-Master clan, watched the beloved Great Forge come to life. A short moment elapsed as if to salute the Great Forge, and he stripped down to the waist to begin his task. His barreled chest and muscular brawn had been hidden by the clothing and armor he wore. Armed with his hammer, tongs, and prods, he approached the anvil and heat source with glee. Retrieving the shards from the original sword, Dabs began to smelt the scandium ore along with the shards. "Biggy, cometh forth and man the bellows!" he shouted. "Quickly now, quickly!" He worked tirelessly for hours on end, shouting occasionally, "Water, more water!" to which SiSi and Smari complied.

Six hours his unstinting arm rose and fell down upon the raw clump of ores, his chest and back drenched in glistening sweat. For three hours more, the blade matured with each dunking of water, back into the molten fires, hammering, dunking. Additional three hours passed with Dabs laboring ceaselessly, with the occasional grindstone passing along the blade and a sporadic dunking of water to whet the grindstone. With a whistle from his lips, Dabs said to no one in particular, "'Tis be done. This be a fine piece of steel, my lad."

"Bring me the hilt!" exclaimed Dabs as he extended his arm behind him without looking. Smari retrieved the hilt and slapped it into the open hand. Like a deft surgeon, he worked on attaching the hilt to the blade. The great sword Mjolnir was reborn! To which Dabs fell to his knees, totally exhausted from his labors.

The group crowded around the motionless Dabs and murmured as one, "Ahhh." They were stunned at the priceless work of art lying atop the anvil. "Donna touch it fer the night, needs to mature!" yelled Dabs.

Agnar touched Dabs on his shoulder and said, "The realm owes ye a great deal for what ye have done this night, my mighty friend. Step one is finished, and I need to depart company for as fast as possible. Step two is to deliver the sword. I will depart in the morrow. We need to camp for the night."

"Aye, me friends, let us rest 'til the morrow," responded Dabbilus.

Stephan and his band were exiting Castle Hearthglen with Baldur, Gagns, Helgi the Gray, and Lady Zonda watching from the castle walls. They were under orders to not engage combat if not attacked. They were to rush as fast as possible to reinforce Fort Windswept. With the column of 125 soldiers, they looked not back as the castle dwindled behind them. At the lead of the column was Stephan, followed by the banner carriers, the archers, the warriors. Trailing behind them were their supplies, which burdened the pack mules.

Baldur turned to his attention toward the Castle Hearthglen's keep where Rikard was readying his thirty troops for their journey to Fort Gate-Pass. A dozen valets were assisting with fastening soldiers with their plate armor. Three valets were using campfire ashes upon the plate armor lest the glint from the sun on their armor would betray them. The castle, now almost devoid of male inhabitants, was almost empty-like. Now the only people he observed were some women and children scurrying about in the streets. Most of the seasoned soldiers were either deployed or about to be stationed throughout the realm. Soon the castle walls will be manned by recruits and youths learning to become soldiers. Commander Foringi, in the companionship of Lieutenant Gagns, and his troops had left earlier last night.

Baldur took off his cloak and placed it upon Lady Zonda since the wind-chill was dropping fast.

"The clouds seem overloaded with dark death, threatening snow today," muttered Baldur to no one in particular. "I wish that the gods will favor them as they reach their destinations."

Turning to Lady Zonda, Baldur grasped her shoulders and said, "At sunrise, I and Helgi the Gray will take flight toward Jotheim. The Gnomish will be of no match against the hordes from the north. Perchance Helgi can talk some sense into King Smakongur."

Lady Zonda paled at the suggestion and bit her lower lip. "Nay! Nay, I forbid you to go," she stammered.

Looking deep into her eyes, Baldur said, "I have to go. My loyalties are to the realm. I am a soldier, not a bureaucrat sitting at the table himself, stuffing food in his mouth, giving orders but never doing anything. I must lead, not sit idly about, and I will not sacrifice one single soldier should I not lead the troops."

Of course, he was correct in his thinking. But Lady Zonda knew also that his decision was the right thing to do, but her frown could not hide her emotions. "Will you wait for me before your departure . . . allow me to say good-bye?" asked Lady Zonda.

Baldur stared for a moment down to the ground then said, "I leave on the morrow before sunrise. Meet us here at the gates, but it is not good-bye, I'll just say 'I will be back soon.'"

Stephan made good speed since he had left Castle Hearthglen. Within the last five hours of the journey, they had found no obstacles or hindrances. The squadron had passed numerous villages that had been left in ruins, the result of the foul hordes' plundering. Countless bodies of orcs, ogres, and men were strewn throughout the fields and dwellings of the villages. Stephan and his men watched stolidly as some villagers were stacking bodies for the pyres. Other villagers, which were the stragglers and survivors, were observed sitting on the roadway as Stephan's column passed. The poor, shocked inhabitants of the village just stared in mute silence to watch the soldiers abandon them. Some of them were swathed in bandages as they attended to their wounds. Stephan halted his journey and helped the poor peasants along the roadway. He instructed the priest within the soldiers' ranks to assist the survivors.

"Hold to the next township where some militia can protect you. We have done all that we can do, we must make way to the front lines," said Stephan. "Go quickly, as the countryside is no man's land."

The village was still smoldering; the clouds of steam escaped into the air. The buzzards were gathering overhead. They will feast well tonight. Stephan knew that it would be folly to dwell on the destruction as the soldiers continued their mission. Devastated and with dwindling hope, Stephan knew that the worst is yet to come.

"Pick up the pace. I fear if we don't reach Bátslipa in time, we will never make our way to Fort Windswept. We need those boats and ferries operational. Bátslipa does have some militia, and we may have to engage combat to rid the ferry passing of the monsters!" yelled Stephan toward his second in command.

Commander Foringi and his crew met with similar sights and circumstances. Every place, there were farmers and peasants strewn on the road. The pleas and cries that engulfed the squad were deafening, with numerous survivors asking if the soldiers could find a lost companion. The troops were hindered by the carts and wagons since the caravan of refugees was vying for the roadway. They were within a two-day march, and they decided to press on over the night. Then and only then did they dare to make camp with the safety of sunrise.

Dabs slept like a rock after the workout at the Great Forge. He shook off the sleep from his eyes, stretched his arms up, and said, "G'day 'til thee."

Agnar had been awake for over an hour before Dabs arose, just staring at the newly formed sword.

"Aye, 'tis it a beauty to behold . . . not bad if ye ask me. I told ya I do good work," added Dabs.

Loftur suddenly intercepted Dabs's praises with "Dabs, ye have a problem. Aye sent darlings out to scout the way out. Thoust me darlings saw hundreds of orcs. Ye be slain within three meters if ye be detected. Me darlings were able to stroll amidst 'em cause the goblins which were within the orcs' gathering."

"It must be because they have reinforced the Eldfjall and the Gates, no other explanation fits," surmised Agnar with disappointment in his voice. "*Now* what? How do we escape? 'Twas this for naught, reforging the sword? We *must* return the sword to its rightful owners!" With that, he strode up to the sword still atop the anvil. As he neared it, the sword hummed to life, and the blade emitted a shimmering golden haze and leapt into his hand. A gust of wind uttering "Mjoooooolniiiiirrrr" lambasted everyone there as if air itself were alive. At the exact time, a tremendous shaking of the earth threw them to the ground, with the shaking of the cavern walls covering them with dust and debris!

"Out! Out!" he shouted as everyone tried to flee. The swaying of the forge caused the people in the cavern to retain their footing like drunken sailors, falling, regaining their stances, falling again. The room had everyone fleeing from the vicinity of the Great Forge before the forge started to collapse. It was as though some invisible force had ignited in the heart of the sword that triggered the tremors. The moment that his hands and the sword met, Agnar felt terrible emotions of both pain and pleasure, as of birthing.

After everyone had regrouped away from the remains of the forge, everyone was coughing from the dust, and the echoes and vibrations and resonances filled the cavern and beyond. The tremors had stopped, and once they had regained their posture, the group scattered about looking for their equipment, which they had brought with them.

"Well," said Dabs. "We still canna find our way back. Best to go back to the village and ponder how to escape." He looked toward Loftur.

Before Loftur could reply, the bleating of horns was heard from the distance. The troop had been spotted, and the noises from the Great Forge had brought with it reinforcements!

"Quickly now, make haste!" commanded Dabs.

Agnar, with Mjolnir now under sheath, ordered Bangsi to appear as he readied his bow.

Biggy did the same with Attafæt, and along with the hunter group, they took a defensive position to cover the fleeing group.

Between the flat blares from the horns, followed by volleys of arrows, Agnar replied with a volley of his own. Bangsi swept into action, targeted the nearest goblin, which resulted in the goblin missing its leg. Agnar discharged an arrow, which cut down an orc. The arrow was protruding out the head of the foe as he fell lifeless. Bangsi was on the back of another orc flailing his mace to no avail as his neck was between the teeth of Bangsi.

"Fall back! Fall back!" yelled Dabs as he assisted the defenders. "Biggy, have Attafæt seal the tunnel once we get through it. It won't hold 'em for long, but long enough."

Agnar recalled Bangsi as the group dodged arrows, trying to make it into the tunnels. Dabs took a glancing arrow in his left arm, to which he snapped in half to prevent hindrance of using his drawn sword. SiSi cast freeze spells upon two of the enemies; Agnar dropped two more foes; Dabs cut down one with a clean swoop of his blade.

"SiSi, use the ward-stone! That can slow the advance!" Biggy yelled.

The band made their way into the tunnel entrance and Attafæt began to spit webs on the ingress area, effectively sealing the door for a bit. The band could hear bleats from the Orcs' horns from beyond the sealed tunnel. Stifled yelling and cursing were heard from beyond the webbing. SiSi drank her last mana potion, inscribed a ward-stone, and placed the stone near the entrance. She conjured a spell to prevent access to the tunnel. In the same instance, Dabs used his lay-on-hand paladin powers along with some mage bandages to heal the wound he had suffered. Loftur and his darlings were in the distance as they were making their way back to his abode to await the others.

After the group had successfully sealed the shaft, they made their way to the old city where Loftur was waiting.

"Loftur, my friend, now is the time to decide. Surely to dwell longer here would invite certain death to you and the darlings," Agnar addressed Loftur. "The webs won't last long, and surely the Orcs have a mage within their group to dispel the ward-stone. They will be in the number of hundreds, nay thousands, once the tunnel is open."

Loftur stared to the ground at his feet. After a few seconds, he responded, "Aye, but *how* dost thou to flee from this place?"

Biggy interceded in a pip-squeaky voice, "Me dost have a plan, a plan that works too!"

Kaldhjarta was standing before the masses of Vithheld. He felt the earlier stabbing pain in his back as the winds bore a low whistled "Mjoooolnirrrr." He had amassed an army before him, decked in the attire of war, listening to the thump of swords against shields.

Standing next to him was Svaramin, his trusted ally, on the balcony. Kaldhjarta knew that something was up and that something had happened that concerned Mjolnir, the great sword. His kingdoms of the north were preparing for open war, and the event of Mjolnir was the omen he was looking for. It would take as planned: attack Jotheim first, with Fort Windswept to be the first victim, then subjugate the lands. The dwarfs would be next, destroying Castle Vokva before Castle Hearthglen could offer assistance to them. The elfin people would be last as they had no long-term relations with the race of man.

He openly smiled upon the smirking Svaramin, taking glee that soon it would be open war. It would be a week-long march before the boats and ferries of Ferjalönd could be reached.

"Within a week then," surmised Svaramin, "within a week, and the south will feel the agony." He smiled, and Svaramin gauged that the mobs below were ready to march toward war; with howls and grunts of pleasure, the masses gathered below were ready. He raised both arms over his head and yelled, "TO WAR! TO WAR! TO WAR!" and took gratification to hear the carnality from the audience.

GLOSSARY

Ápstil—Race of humanoids dark brown in color known for its riding steeds. Ruthless and cunning, they are bedouin in nature.

Attafæt—Biggy's giant konglo.

Aura—Monetary amount (one hundred aura = ten- sheckles).

Bangsi—Agnar's wolverine sekhmet.

Blafjall—Mountains just south of Fort Hermana.

Bleusgrof—Farm owned by Biggy.

Closu—Agnar's horse.

Castle Hearthglen—Capital for the humans.

Dabbilus—Dwarven paladin, called Dabs for short.

Dragonhead Inn—Inn in the Fort Gate-Pass village.

Dwarfs—Stunted humanoid with extraordinary strength. Generally, they live underground and create magnificent things using a hammer and chisel. They work ores and gems from the ground, use forges, and are excellent armor producers.

Einauga—Cyclops in the forge.

Elves—Race of inhabitants, pale skinned with pointy ears. They are attuned to nature itself.

Ferjalönd—Ferry and ports on the north. ferreter— Hunter by trade in the military.

Foringi—Second in command at Ft. Hermana.

Flugarpets—Flying mounts.

Gemshard Heart—Precious gems that are used to bolster armor.

Gnomes—Knee-high (to human) race that use science to invent. They are good in accounting as well as in banking.

Goblins—Race of creatures (similar to dwarf in size) that is excellent working with the sciences. They are dark-green-skinned with pointy ears and no hair.

Gormur—Lead architect for Jarnsmiða Forge.

Gufaheita—Steam-generated hot pits around geothermal areas.

Hearthglen—The ruling castle of the race of men.

Heitapipur—Steam pipes used by dwarfs in their forges.

Helgi the Gray—Snjofell after he was slain.

Hestur—Mounts (can be horses, donkeys, cattle, eagles, in the case of good characters. Can be fiery steeds, mountain goats, water buffalo, bats, Roks in the case of evil).

Humans—Race of people that are generally tall and good at military skills, organizational skills.

Kaldhjarta—Ruler of Vithheld, a dark, evil protagonist.
konglo—Spiders, giant web-weaving creatures.
komdu—Order for the sekhmet to appear.

Jarnsmiða Forge—Dwarven iron forge factory.

Jokla City—North Alliance city inhabited by orcs and trolls and ogres.

Joldugrof—Farm north of Egilsstað.

Loftur Hamarsson—Iron-forging dwarf in the forge.
  mage bandages—Used by healers and constructed
  by bolts of mage cloth.

Magnus—King of Jarnsmiða.

Mjolnir—The great sword forged by the dwarfs.
  ogres—Race of huge heavy-set bodies, muscular
  with two fangs protruding from their lower jaw.
  They are rather slow intellectually and hard to
  agonize.

Orcs—Race that is aggressive and militarized. They
  have a greenish-hued skin, generally with two
  fangs protruding from their lower jaw. Almost
  always with a crop of black hair braided on the
  head.

Ormskepna—Evil adviser.

Rikard—Dwarf prisoner.

Salim-Dug—'Apstil commander.

Sekhmet—Pet (can be cats, dogs, wolverines, bat,
  apes).

Scandium—The great ore given by Thor for forging
  the great sword Mjolnir.

Shiva—Sphinx of Jarnsmiða.

SiSi—Biggy's girlfriend.

Skelbaka—Outpost for the North Alliance.

Smakongur—King of the Gnomish people and the
  Kingdom Jotheim.

Sko Forest Forest area where Elves live

Stephan—Prisoner who befriended Baldur.

Svartaturn—The new black tower used by Svaramin.

Ten-sheckles—Monetary amount used.

Two-Fishes Inn—Tavern in Castle Vokva.

Trolls—Race of inhabitants similar to ogres, usually used in manual labor.

Vithheld—The castle of Kaldhjarta.